# EROS

GW01418689

## Book 1

## Rope

Dante Remy

Illustrated by Reina Canalla

Copyright 2024 by Erosetti Press | All Rights Reserved - Inquiries:
ISBN 978-1-964194-28-8 | danteremy.com & reinacanallaart.com

**Erosetti Press** *Let us journey. together*

ErosettiPress.com

# Erosetti

## *Let us journey together*

**Erosetti | noun |** : an interwoven art form of erotica, vignette, and media creating a captivating and intimate experience. A term coined to describe original works and collaborations with artists who share a passion for exploring the depths of human desire and sensuality.

Erosetti Press is a niche publisher representing artists, writers, and creators who weave erotic, written, and visual media to create immersive audience experiences. Publishing print trade books and e-books, art prints, and limited-edition books, each publication is a journey into human desire and sensuality. *Let us journey together*

# Erosetti Press

# Erosetti
## Book VI

## Rope

## Introduction

The public life of decency and respect,
And the expectations of others,
That monitor my existence,
Fade away.

"Rope" invites you to journey into the intimate and complex interplay of control, freedom, pain, and pleasure. I share this narrative with you with the hope of conveying the depths of human emotions and desires through the lens of erotica.

At its core, "Rope" explores the quintessential human desire for control and the paradoxical freedom found within its constraints. The narrator's carefully chosen rope symbolizes a profound yearning for surrender. This act of surrender is a conscious decision, a testament to trust and vulnerability. It represents a relinquishment of control, allowing another to guide and shape the experience, reflecting the idea that true freedom often comes from understanding and embracing our limitations.

Another central theme in "Rope" is the intricate relationship between pain and pleasure. As the narrator describes her sensations, a tapestry of dualities is expressed, heightening the erotic experience. These words, paired with the evocative illustrations of Reina Canalla, suggest embracing discomfort can lead to profound personal transformation.

Trust is a fundamental element woven throughout "Rope," providing a unique and powerful foundation for the erotic narrative. The narrator's willingness to be bound and controlled is rooted in deep trust and intimacy with their partner. This trust allows for a vulnerable yet empowering exchange, where boundaries are pushed, and deeper connections are forged.

Thank you for joining me on this journey. I hope "Rope" resonates with you, offering both an exploration of deep, intimate desires and a reflection on the broader human experience.

**The Erosetti Book Series**, like pillow books of Japanese antiquity, unfold tales of sensuality, delving into the profound intricacies of fantasies, sharing their depth with others. Whether bestowed upon a lover, a confidant, or nestled into your personal library, these short-format books speak the language of passion. Silence spells the demise of the erotic. Your purchase, gift, and enjoyment of an Erosetti book represents a journey into shared pleasure. *Let us journey together.*

Dante Remy

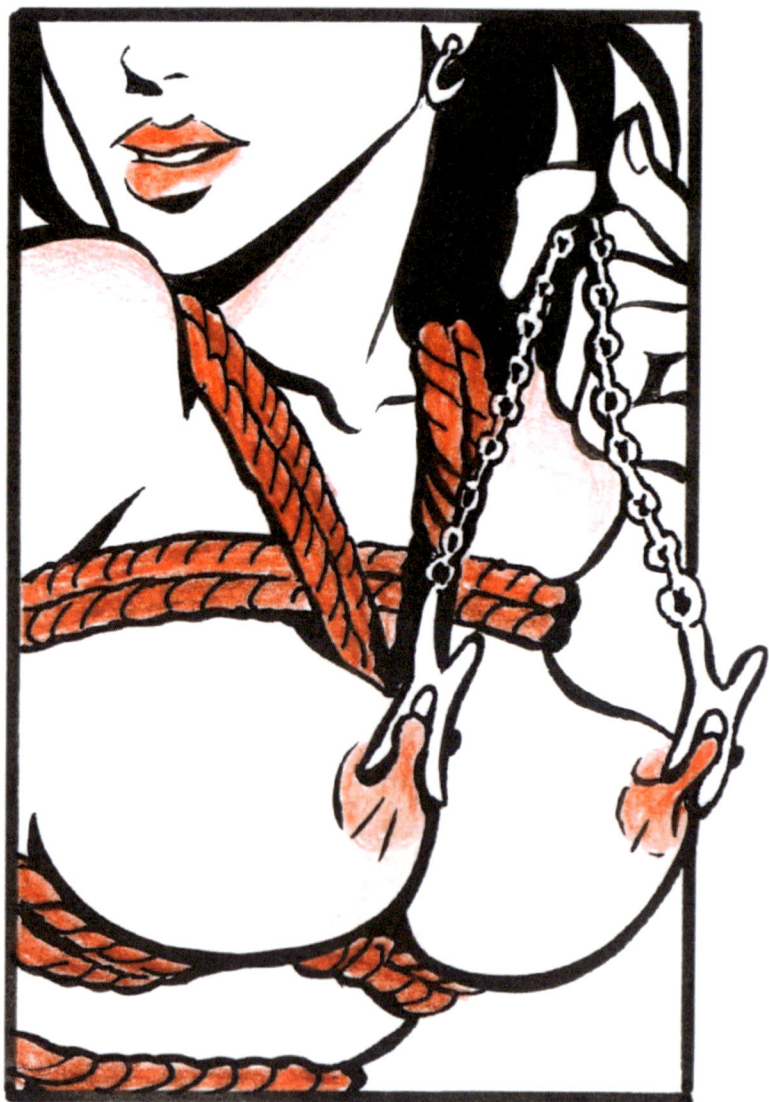

# Rope

Dante Remy

Rope.
You chose it for me so carefully.
Thoughtfully.
Even its color.
You love the look of its deep red,
Against my skin.
It is thick and soft.
Its braids hold me tightly, firmly.
Turns of the rope press into my skin,
but never hurt.
I love the feeling of being bound by it,
And restrained for you to use me.
It binds together so many sensations.
You use them all on me,
Because I need this.
I need you to own me,
And to give me everything I deserve.

I've stared at the bottom drawer for hours.
That's where the rope sits.
An empty drawer, save for this thick, red coil.
When you're away, the desire for it grows.
I watch the drawer from the corner of my eye.
I pace the room during my daily routine.
Nothing breaks its spell.
My need grows.
It burns in me.
Finally, I reach down, open,
And take it from its keep.

Bringing the rope to my face,
I inhale, trying to detect a lingering memory.
I place it on the kitchen island,
Where you will see it when you return,
And I wait.
I go through the motions of the day.
Thoughts of tasks give me momentary relief.
Stopping in a trance,
A hand lingers down my cotton dress,
Pressing the fabric against my panties.
I am wet for hours, in anticipation.
I could touch myself and cum instantly,
Thinking about the pleasure you give me,
But it wouldn't satisfy me.
I'd feel empty and embarrassed.
I need you to take me;
To give me more than release.
I need you to control me:
To take me outside myself;
To separate body from mind;
And, then, put me back together,
Giving me pleasure that is beyond myself.

I hear the door open.
I know you've seen it.
You walk past me,
Giving my flushing cheek a peck.
A friendly greeting on the way to the shower.
I am always bewildered by your way.
So relaxed. So warm.
How do you flip that switch?
I stumble my way through final tasks of
the day,
Listening to the shower run,
Thinking about the water running over your body.
I am lost in these passing minutes.

When I enter the bedroom,
You are drying off, warm and moist.
My mind is blank.
You speak in single words.

"Rope."

I instantly feel my wetness grow,
And the familiar ache between my legs.
The word snaps me back,
To the here and now.
I leave to retrieve it,
And return like a cat delivery its prey,
At the foot of its owner.
You tell me to undress.
My dress and panties,
Wet from waiting,
Fall to the floor.
You toss the towel from your hips,
Onto the desk chair.

"Sit."

I pick up the rope,
And sit down on the simple wooden chair,
Feeling the towel under me,
Warm from your body.
You stand in front of me, naked.
My eyes are on yours.
I want to look down,
To study your cock as it grows,
But your eyes hold mine,
And the wait nearly drives me over the edge.
My breathing increase,
And my nipples are hard.
Anticipating that word again.

"Rope."

I offer it to you,
My eyes never leaving yours.
I press my legs together,
And a rush of wetness fills the space,
Between my legs.

You accept the rope,
And move behind me.

"Arms."

I drape them behind the back of the chair.
As the rope begins to twist and turn,
Around my arms.
Your breath is warm and steady,
Contrasting with my sighs and faint moans.
It's a rhythmic pattern of ties and knots.
My body reacts to every light tug,
As my arms are methodically bound.
The pressure on my arms is overcome,
By the ache of my nipples,
Pushed forward as my back is arched,
And lines of pleasure racing down to my pussy,
Wet as it moves against the towel.
These sensations alone,
Can bring me to orgasm.
But, you've only started.

Being bound by this rope,
Held in place by it, releases me.
When you take me this way,
I find my inner voice.
It's primal. It's loud.
My moans fill the space,

Between mind and body.
All norms of behavior are removed.
The public life of decency and respect,
And the expectations of others,
That monitor my existence,
Fade away.
I need this.
I need this to be released.
To be released into ecstasy.
We've found what taps directly into my core.
You give this to no one else but me.
It's mine.
I'm yours.
I'll cum so hard straining against the rope.
It holds me together when I've lost,
Complete and utter control.

You remain behind me,
Taking a long moment to admire your work.
I can barely take the touch of your fingers,
Tracing down and around my shoulders.
Reaching to my hard nipples.
My eyes closed,
Head thrown back,
The lightest of caresses make me moan,
Long and deep.
I've waited all day for this.
Touch. Caress. Tease.
When you take each of my nipples,
Between your forefinger and thumb,
I drench the towel.
I can barely breathe.
Any air I manage to take in,
Quickly escapes my lungs as a sound of
pleasure.
You sense I'm close,
And squeeze and pinch harder.

I slide my pussy over the towel,
Hoping to touch my clit.
I'm right there.
Closer.
Fuck.
Yes.

You abruptly stop.
But my body resists recovering,
Slowly receding from orgasm.
I need more.
I sense you behind me.
Watching me.
My breathing becomes more regular,
But I am ready,
And I crave what I hear.
A drawer opening.
The clicking of a thin chain,
Attached to clamps.
Your hard cock grazes my arm.
A nipple is pinched between metal,
And fixed in place by a small ring,
Raised and secured to ensure no relief.
Then the other,
Fixed in the perpetual pinch of the clamp.
The chain drapes downward in a loop,
Teasing my nipples as it moves.
Your hand caresses my inner thigh.
You put pressure on the chain,
Just light enough,
To send a throbbing mix of pain and pleasure,
From my nipples,
To my clenching pussy.

At first, I cannot moan.
My mouth opens wide.
I try to breathe.
Your hand touches my wetness.
Two fingers enter me deep.
Then, begin to slowly exit.
Your fingers curl deliberately upwards,
Passing over my prized flower,
That deepest pleasure center,
Forcing me to finally release a gasp.
But I must wait.

Your wet fingers on my lips,
Invite me to taste.
I take them into my mouth,
Savoring with my tongue what I've given you,
With licks and wet clicks.
Satisfied, your reach moves down again.
Tracing with your fingertips,
Tension on the chain.,
Lower.
Anticipating your touch,
Brings me so close,
Once again.

A single middle finger reaches my clit.
You increase tension on the chain.
A dull ache overcomes the touch,
As my pussy contracts.
Each time your finger moves,
Up and down on my clit,
You increase the tension.
I want you to pull harder.
I want to feel each clamp tease and pull,
And cut through the pleasure on my clit.

The longer you draw this out,
This pain and pleasure,
The deeper I fall into myself.
My eyes closed.
My mouth widens.
Gasps and sounds of want and need,
Escape with each touch,
Each ache.
Faster.
Harder.
Fuck, I want more.
Your finger dances over my clit,
As I arch to increase the tension,
Of your hold.

This exchange builds,
Touch and tension,
Pleasure and pain,
Until you rhythmically bring me to orgasm.
I no longer feel with one part of my body.
I am cumming.
All of me.
I won't remember this.
When I try,
I simply shudder,
Knowing I came harder,
Than my mind and body comprehend.

Coming down from orgasm,
A hard slap on my ass brings me back.
You've stood me up,
And bent me over the chair.
The palm of your hand strikes again.
This time, on the other cheek.

I've not fully recovered.
The need to cum again grows.
I arch my back and offer you my ass.
I need this.
More than anything,
I need you to bring this out of me.
Each strike is met by a contraction,
Deep inside my pussy.
Even the touch of your fingertips.
On my glowing skin,
Makes my pussy involuntarily ache.
Your hand, holding the inside of my thigh,
Braces me for another strike.
It's loud and snaps against my skin.
I feel the familiar struggle,
Rise within me.
With each strike,
My ass burns for more,
Dowsed by my aching,
Drenched pussy,
Heightened still by the hand holding me.
The grasp on my thigh inches upwards,
Until I feel a finger against my wetness.

As your other hand gives me,
Momentary reprieve,
Tracing red marks on my skin,
Two fingers enter me deeply,
Fingers curled upwards.
Finding my pleasure center.
I arch my hips,
Begging to be stroked.
Begging to be released.

My moans are uncontrollable.
You touch the deepest part of me.
My body moves with you.
Devouring your fingers placed so perfectly.
You resume the strikes on my ass.
With each spank,
My pussy grips your fingers tightly,
Bracing for another,
Before my mind can catch up,
To these sensations.

I moan louder.
The rope binding my arms releases me,
Forces me to let go.
Another slap, hard, on my ass.
I moan louder.
Your stroking quickens.

Slap.

Fuck. Right there.
My legs shake.
My body tenses.

Slap.

Harder.
I drench your fingers.
I clench hard.
Harder on my deepest flower.

Slap.

My entire body is cumming.

Slap. Slap. Slap.

Every strike on my ass pushes my orgasm,
Further into my soul.
I cum in waves,
Feeling everything at once.
A fog moves over my mind.
I am m lost in pleasure.
I am a tightly bound package,
Made to cum.

Your arms envelop me.
I am led to the edge of the bed.
Bent over.
Shaking uncontrollably,
My body will not release me from this pleasure.
My face is buried in the sheets.
Your hands on my hips.

"Fuck me."

"Fuck me.", I shudder.

Your cock enters me,
Wet, tight, wanting.
I moan, taking every inch,
Until you are deep inside me.

"Fuck me." I beg.

I moan with the first strokes of your cock.
You fuck me hard.
Your breath is desperate.
My body pushes my mind aside.
I pulse around your cock,
Gripping it,
Releasing it,
Matching your rhythm.
I am outside myself with pleasure.

My orgasm is revived,
As I climax again.
You take short breaths between gasps.
Your cock hardens.
You dig your fingers into my hips,
Fucking me harder as you release,
Cumming deep inside me,
With long, hard thrusts.
Your cock is buried inside me.
My body shaking,
Feels your chest against my back.
Your kisses run down on my neck.
We breathe together.

Kneeling between my legs,
You begin unwinding the rope.
Each turn and pull brings me back.
Casting it aside,
Your hands grasp my arms at the shoulders,
And pull downwards,
To my wrists,
Bringing a warm and inviting bliss,
Through my arms.

Your fingers caress my red-hot skin,
And remaining imprints of the rope.
You admire your work.
I arch my ass and smile,
As your touch moves over my body.
I am yours.
You collapse over me,
And bury your face,
Into my arms.

I will carry this glow for days.

I will press the palms of my hands,
Over my breasts,
And feel the ache of my nipples.

Cool water will tickle the red marks,
On my skin.

I will shudder,
Remembering glimpses of my orgasm.

And the rope?
The red, thick, soft rope,
Will sit in the bottom drawer,
Waiting patiently,
Until I cannot.
Until I need it.
To be released,
Once again.

.

# Rope

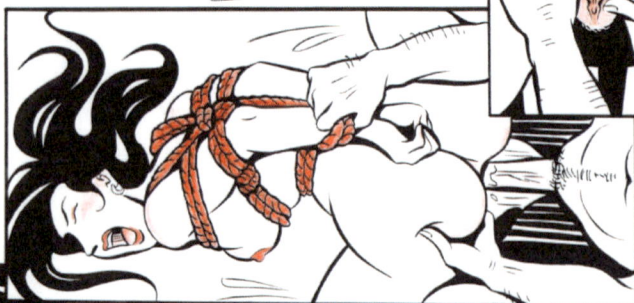

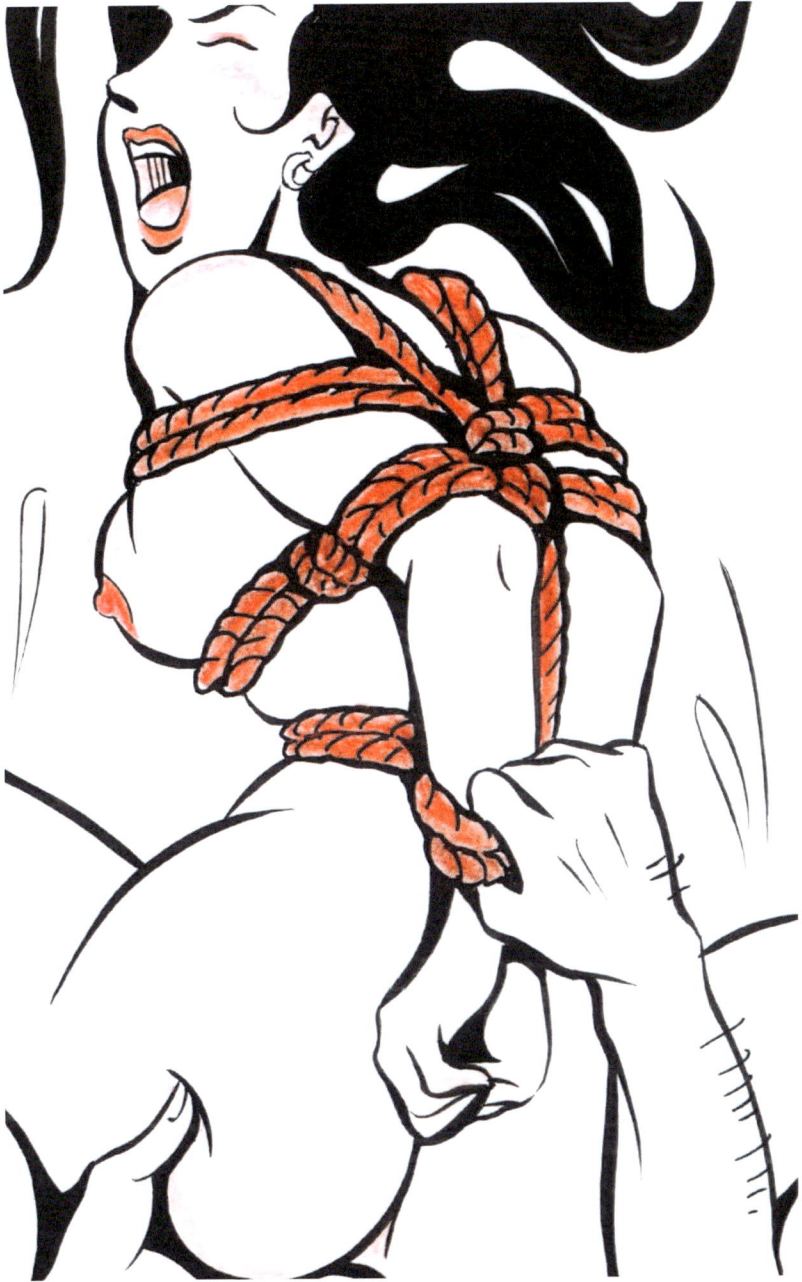

# About the Author & Artist

Dante Remy is an internationally-based writer and creator. His work explores the aesthetic in the everyday and the search for humanity through word and visualizatiom. Running themes explore: the duality of nature and science, love and loss, beauty and the macabre, the chaste and the erotic. The Erosetti pillow book series marks his inaugural venture into published print erotica, seamlessly melding his distinct visual writing style with interpretations by skilled artists. His comprehensive portfolio can be explored at danteremy.com.

Reina Canalla is a Spanish author, artist, and illustrator who studied drawing and painting at Carme Muset Art Academy and comic book illustration at Joso School. Canalla has won several awards for her work, including the Barcelona International Comic Fair Award and the Erotica Comics Award. In addition to her art, she has authored the novel Las Vírgenes de Nuria, available in Spanish at Amazon Kindle. Her celebrated erotic comic series, Anne-Marie, A shameless and erotic pirate comic, is available at reinacanallaart.com and in deluxe hardcover and paperback editions at ErosettiPress.com. Her latest project is the erotic comic Mademoiselle D'Artagnan.

Conceptual Sketch by Reina Canalla, July 2024

# More Books in the Erosetti Series

## EROSETTI
## Book I

## Black Choker

ISBN 979-8-9896305-1-6
Available at ErosettiPress.com
and all major online and local
bookstores.

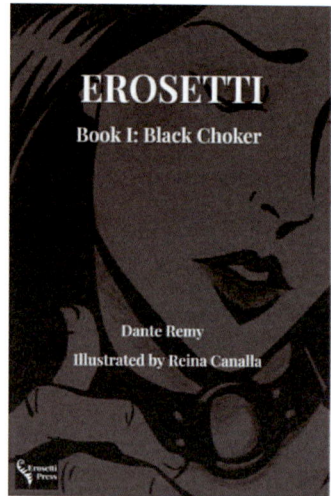

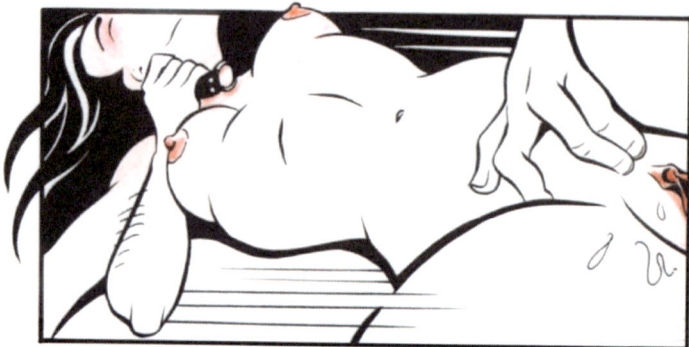

# More Books in the Erosetti Series

## EROSETTI
## Book II

# I Don't Know You. You Don't Know Me.

ISBN 979-8-9896305-4-7
Available at ErosettiPress.com
and all major online and local
bookstores.

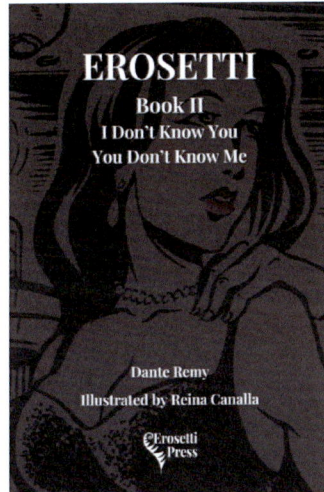

# More Books in the Erosetti Series

## EROSETTI
## Book III

## The Impression

ISBN 978-1-964194-01-1
Available at ErosettiPress.com
and all major online and local
bookstores.

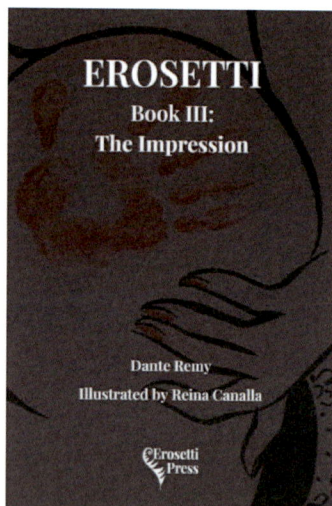

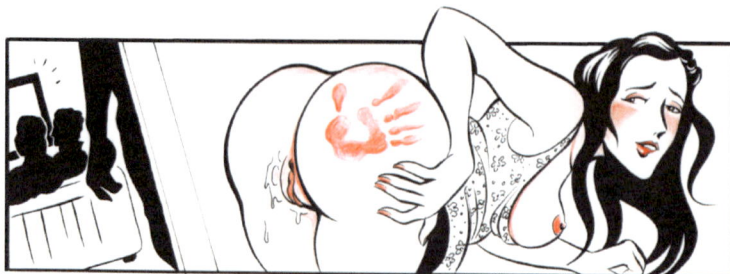

# More Books in the Erosetti Series

## EROSETTI
## Book IV

## Catharsis

ISBN 978-1-964194-03-5
Available at ErosettiPress.com
and all major online and local
bookstores.

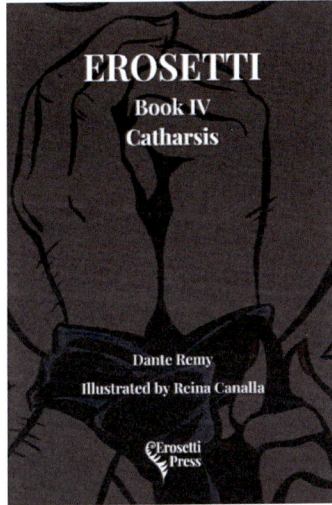

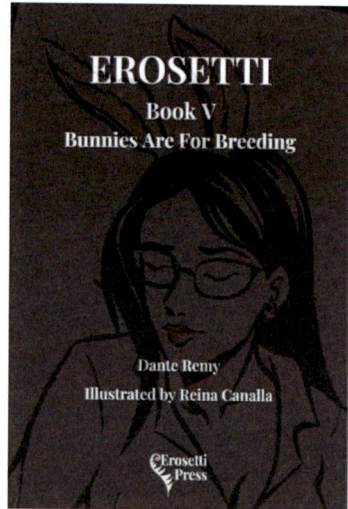

# New from Reina Canalla

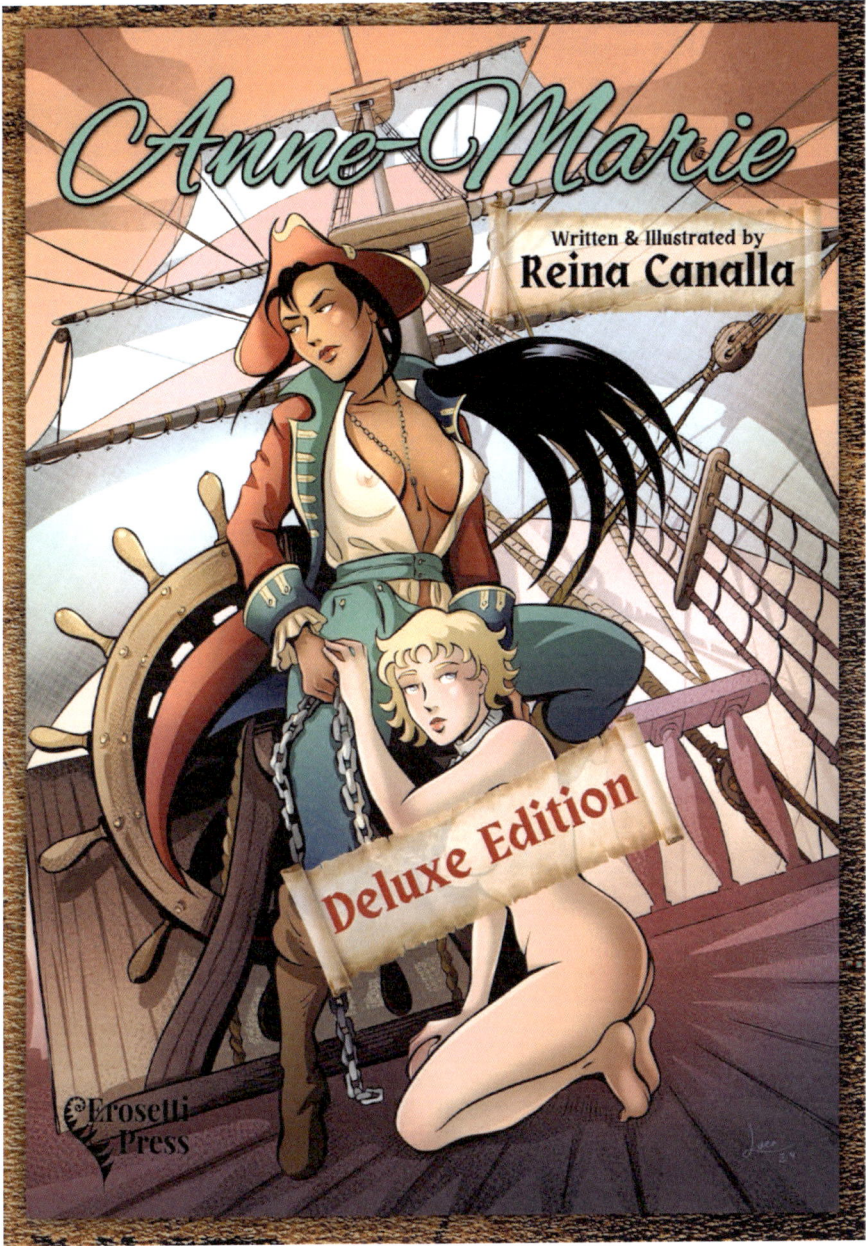

Anne-Marie

Written & Illustrated by
**Reina Canalla**

Deluxe Edition

Eroselli Press

Milton Keynes UK
Ingram Content Group UK Ltd.
UKRC030823270824
447493UK00007B/20